Reign On!

Adapted by Maggie Fischer

from the series *Elena of Avalor*, created by Craig Gerber

Based on *Elena of Avalor: King of the Carnaval*
written by Craig Gerber and Tom Rogers

Avalor's Carnaval is based on a festival held in Bolivia and other Latin American countries that fills the streets with marching bands and dancers.

It's time for Carnaval in the Kingdom of Avalor, and Elena and her family are making preparations for the royal float!

Isabel takes charge of the construction, and Armando asks Elena to gather some extra flowers for decoration. Happy to help, she starts off for the courtyard with a basket full of colorful flowers to add to their float.

Excited to see all of the beautiful floats that are being prepared for the parade, Elena hurries, shoes slapping on the cobblestone floor. When she enters the courtyard, she runs into a giant Maruvian phoenix! Elena is so startled that she drops her basket and her flowers fly everywhere!

Though she is confident and decisive, sometimes Elena can be impulsive and leaps before she looks.

With another glance, she realizes that the phoenix is actually made of papier-mâché. What a relief! The head wobbles and moves to the side to reveal . . . Esteban?

Got you, Elena!

"It's so good to see you in the Carnaval spirit, Esteban!" Elena giggles.

You look just like your mother when you laugh.

I do?

"Carnaval was Mami's favorite holiday," Elena notes wistfully, starting to pick up the fallen flowers. Esteban joins in, handing the phoenix beak to Higgins.

"Yes, riding with you and your mother on the royal float was one of my last happy memories . . ." Esteban's face falls.

. . . Before the dark times.

Elena squeezes his hand to pull him out of his sad memory. "That's why I brought Carnaval back to the kingdom, cousin," she tells him.

Now we can make more good memories

4

Esteban takes the papier-mâché beak back from Higgins, and they join the rest of the family who are busy getting the float ready for the parade.

Isabel looks up from the float's blueprints and brightens. "You have the beak! Great!"

"Yes, now where does it go?" Esteban teases. Isabel gapes at him. Where did this playful Esteban come from, she wonders. He helps her place the beak on the float.

"I think I know who should be King of the Carnaval this year, Isa," says Elena, leaning her head toward Esteban.

Isabel nods in agreement, smiling, and the rest of the family starts voicing their agreement.

The King of the Carnaval gets to announce the start of the parade and officially begin the Carnaval.

N-no, no. I am not worthy of such an honor.

Just think about it, okay?

"Now, where's Armando?" Elena asks, looking around at the float. "He wanted these flowers."

At the sound of his name, Armando pokes his head out of the side of the phoenix. "Right here, your highness!"

Armando's movement causes the phoenix beak to pop out of its place on the float and bounce off the side and onto Esteban's head!

Oh no, the beak!

"Armando!" Esteban yells, his voice muffled as he tries to get the phoenix off of his head.

"Sorry!" Armando winces.

Old Friends

Esteban finally gets the phoenix beak off his head when he hears a shout across the courtyard.

Avalor is built upon the ruins of the ancient civilization that was known as Maru.

El Segundo!

Victor?

Victor approaches, saying, "So you do remember me, El Segundo?"

"Actually, it's *Chancellor* Esteban now," says Esteban with his chin up.

"That's a very nice chicken mask," chuckles Victor.

"It's a phoenix!" snaps Esteban. "And this is not a mask."

Victor pulls Esteban in for a hug, still laughing. When he is close to Esteban, Victor hisses, "After what you did to me, I would have thought you'd be too ashamed to show your face."

"Princess Elena, you are more beautiful than ever."

"Have we met?"

Elena's grandmother Luisa loves to cook, and everyone adores her *tamales* and *calabaza en tacha*.

Victor bends into a sweeping bow.

"It was forty-one years ago, before Shuriki invaded," Victor answers, looking solemn. I am sure I look very different now. Back then, my father was the Royal Treasurer."

"Victor *Delgado*?" Elena asks, realizing.

Victor nods and smiles. They are soon joined by Francisco and Luisa, who are delighted to see Victor again.

"It has been too long, Victor!" exclaims Francisco, giving him a hug.

"Better check your pockets, Abuelo," Esteban warns.

Victor moves his hand from Francisco's pocket and reveals his empty palm, then opens his other hand, where Francisco's medal was hiding! He winks, giving the medal back to Francisco.

Francisco chuckles, saying, "Just like old times, with you and Esteban! Always practicing your sleight-of-hand tricks!"

"Tricks, yes," Luisa replies, laughing. "That was their excuse for taking things that didn't belong to them."

Abuelo means *grandfather* in Spanish.

Victor introduces his daughter, Carla, to the Flores family.

"It's a pleasure to meet you all, I've heard so much about you," Carla says brightly.

"Where have you been all these years?" Elena asks.

Victor sighs. "When Shuriki took over, we had to flee the kingdom. Now that Avalor is free, I want to show Carla where I grew up!"

"And to celebrate Carnaval, of course!" Carla adds.

"Yes, how wonderful that you've brought back the old traditions . . . we must never forget the past," Victor says, looking at Esteban.

When Shuriki was the ruler of Avalor, she banned all music, dancing, and magic that wasn't her own, which meant the citizens couldn't hold Carnaval.

Elena decides to make the Delgados her personal guests for the Carnaval that day.

"First, could we get a tour of the palace?" asks Carla. "I've never seen anything so beautiful!"

Of course! I'll show you around myself.

Esteban decides to join them, so he can keep an eye on Victor.

"Higgins! Come along," Esteban says. They rush after Elena and their new guests as they head into the palace.

It was Esteban who stole Shuriki's wand so that Elena could destroy it and finally defeat the sorceress.

Avalor is adorned with wonderful plants and scented flowers that wrap around railings and the palace courtyard.

"I can't believe you grew up here, Papá!" Carla gasps.

"El Segundo grew up here; I was just a visitor," Victor replies.

"Why do you call Esteban "El Segundo," Victor?" Elena asks.

"When we were young we used to race all over the place, and Esteban always came in *second*!" Victor chuckles.

An annoyed Esteban tries to end the tour early, but Carla wants to see the Treasury where her grandfather worked. Esteban tries to protest, but Elena gives in.

"It'll only take a few minutes, Esteban. Summon the Captain of the Guard," Elena calls out.

The Captain of the Guard uses his keys to unlock the Treasury, and the group rushes inside.

"We have the best security system in the world! Isabel helped set it up," Elena explains to the guests.

Princess Isabel is an inventor—she aspires to create many useful things!

"Your little sister?" Victor replies, surprised. Elena nods, smiling.

Carla gazes in awe at the silver platters, gold chalices, and jewels that line the walls of the Treasury.

This is all *yours?*

"It belongs to the kingdom of Avalor. We are just the caretakers," Elena answers.

On Elena's 15th birthday, her mother gave her the amulet that ended up saving her life.

Elena makes her way to the front of the Treasury.

"This one is my favorite," she tells Carla. Elena points to a spectacular jeweled tiara that rests on the head of a mannequin dressed in royal finery.

It was my mother's.

"But she only wore it at Carnaval. I remember how it used to sparkle in the sun . . ."

Elena flashes back to a memorable
Carnaval with her mother.

"One time, when I was eight, she even let
me wear that tiara. I was the happiest girl in all
of Avalor that day," Elena states, dreamily.

Elena's
full name
is Elena
Castillo
Flores.

I'll never forget how we
used to ride together
on the float.

Princess Isabel has a very scientific mind, and prefers to calculate and consider all of the outcomes before making a decision.

"The tiara is beautiful," Carla says, gazing at it.

"It's even prettier up close! Let's check it out!" Elena says excitedly.

"Be careful, Elena! It's not safe!" Esteban intervenes.

"Oh, right, I almost forgot! The whole room is booby-trapped," Elena explains to Victor and Carla.

Esteban clears his throat. "Let's go back downstairs, I'm sure Isabel needs our help finishing the float."

The Captain of the Guard locks the Treasury door behind the visitors, but as he turns, he accidentally runs into Carla, and they fall down in a heap.

Victor helps Carla up, and she sneakily shows him the key to the Treasury she stole from the Captain when she "fell."

One of the rising stars of the Royal Guard is a guard named Gabe, one of Elena's close friends.

I'm so sorry! I thought we were going *that* way!

Entirely my fault, señorita!

As the tour group heads back to the courtyard, Victor whispers to Carla, "Remember the plan: you keep them distracted while I steal the jewels."

Carla nods discreetly, then calls out to Elena.

Isabel hands Carla a paintbrush. "There's one for Señor Delgado, too!"

"Oh, I would love to, but I am very tired from the trip," Victor replies.

If you need any help with the float, I'm happy to lend a hand!

"Well, if you're tired, Avalor City has many fine inns," Esteban comments nastily.

Elena rolls her eyes. "Esteban, there are only a million rooms in the palace. Armando?"

Armando turns around swiftly, knocking the beak off of the phoenix again. "Yes, princess?"

"Could you please show Victor to the parlor?" Elena asks Armando.

"No need, your highness," Victor replies smoothly. "I spent my childhood in these halls—I know the way."

Two flying jaquins are featured on the Royal Family crest.

Esteban attempts to follow Victor into the palace, but Isabel stops him.

"Cousin Esteban, could you help put the beak back on the float?" she asks. Esteban sighs and turns to help.

Before he puts the beak back on, Esteban pulls Higgins to the side.

"Follow him, Higgins. I do not trust him," Esteban says.

"But you've known him for ages," Higgins protests.

That is how I know he is up to no good.

Higgins follows Victor as best he can, but his sneaking skills could use some work. He hides behind potted palms, and takes cover behind statues.

As Higgins rounds the corner, he bumps right into Victor!

"Were you following me?" Victor asks suspiciously.

"Me? No! I was just going to . . . uh . . . the . . ." Higgins stammers.

"To the kitchen?" Victor finishes for him.

"Yes, the kitchen," Higgins mumbles.

"Great! Perhaps you can fetch me a torta. I am very hungry. In fact, fetch yourself one while you're at it," Victor orders.

"Thanks, Victor! I could use a snack! I'll meet you in the parlor."

A torta is a kind of sandwich, served on a crusty sandwich roll.

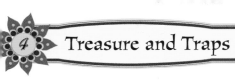

With Higgins distracted, Victor hurries to the Treasury and unlocks the door with the stolen key.

He gazes at all the jewels and starts toward them when a glint catches his eye. Kneeling down, he discovers that it is ⸺ ⸺ re, hooked up ⸺ a series of bells.

The palace kitchen is always busy, and uses a stone oven for traditional cooking.

You call this a security system? Child's play.

Victor continues into the room after stepping over the tripwire, and the floor tile gives way under his foot. **POP! POP! POP!**

The pressure-plate floor tiles tug on a wire that causes a blowpipe to start firing hot pink dye right at Victor!

When Shuriki took over the Kingdom of Avalor, it was Alcazar, the Royal Wizard, who saved Elena and her family by putting them inside the Amulet of Avalor and the magic painting.

Meanwhile, Higgins comes back in the courtyard, eating a ham and cheese torta and holding the second torta on a plate.

Esteban comes up to him and demands, "Where is Victor?"

"I wish I knew. I have his torta," Higgins replies calmly.

"What?! I told you to follow him, not to fix him a snack! Give me that!" Esteban snaps.

Victor appears in the courtyard, scrubbed clean. Smiling, he passes by Esteban and grabs the torta from him.

There's my torta. Thanks, El Segundo.

"I have had enough of your games, Victor. What are you *really* doing here?"

"Just visiting old friends," Victor replies smugly.

Esteban looks at him suspiciously and notices a pink splotch of paint on his shirtsleeve.

You tried to steal the royal jewels!

Victor looks at Esteban coldly.

"This is nothing compared to what you did to me," Victor responds.

Esteban begins to look guilty, and so Victor continues talking.

"Forty-one years ago, you and I made a deal with Shuriki. We were going to help her invade Avalor and rule the kingdom with her. We were *partners*. But when Shuriki kicked me and my family out of Avalor, you did nothing to stop her," Victor finishes, looking furious.

When Esteban destroyed Shuriki's wand, the veil of eternal youth was lifted, and she turned into an old woman.

Esteban looks guilty, and runs a hand down his face, sighing.

"What could I do? You saw what she did to Elena's parents. That was not part of the plan! Then she told me to serve her or else. I had no choice," Esteban pleads with Victor.

You always have a choice.

Victor looks over at Esteban's family building the royal float for the parade together, and smirks, gesturing to them.

"For example, I could *choose* to tell your family that you betrayed them all," Victor threatens.

Or I could choose to keep your secret.

As Elena is working on the float, she notices how tense the conversation seems to be between Victor and Esteban, and grows concerned.

She starts to descend the ladder to walk toward the men, but Carla knocks the float's beak loose again and drapes it over herself, crying:

Oh, clumsy me! Elena, can you help me?

Elena rushes over to help Carla.

Esteban pleads with Victor not to reveal to his family that he's a traitor.

"Oh, I won't. *If* you steal me the Crown Jewels," Victor says. "I couldn't get past the booby traps, but I'm sure you know every *inch* of that Treasury. Bring me the jewels . . . or I tell them your secret," Victor says menacingly.

Long ago, Elena was freed from her amulet with the help of Sofia, another young princess from a neighboring kingdom, Enchancia.

Pale and anxious with worry that his family will discover his terrible secret, Esteban goes to the Royal Treasury to follow through with his promise to Victor. The Captain of the Guard passes by and waves to Esteban in welcome.

"Get ahold of yourself. It's either this, or they find out the truth," Esteban mutters to himself.

Esteban breathes in deeply and enters the Treasury.

As Esteban enters the room, the first thing he sees is the Flores family portrait from forty-one years ago, and he is overcome with guilt.

Nevertheless, he hops over trip-wires, dodges pink dust-bombs, and swerves around giant boulders and swinging axes as he makes his way past the booby traps and deeper into the Treasury.

Esteban used to believe his family did not care for him, and his loneliness and quest for power caused him to join forces with Shuriki and betray those closest to him.

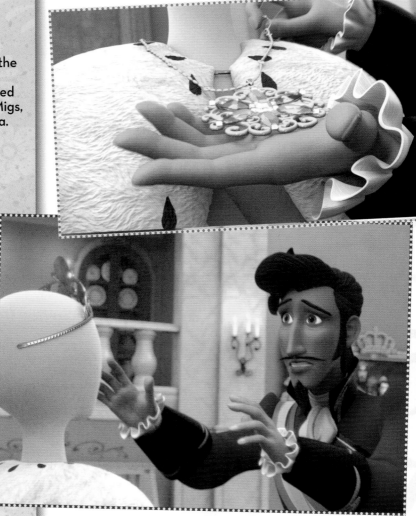

As he makes his way past the last of the booby traps, Esteban begins to grab the Crown Jewels and stuff them into his satchel.

He glances at Elena's mother's tiara, and hesitates for a moment.

Sighing, he takes that too, and starts to leave the room.

As he leaves the Treasury, Esteban runs smack into Elena!

"I've been looking all over for you," Elena begins, "It's time to go to the parade." She pauses as she notices the tiara in his hands.

> What are you doing with my mother's tiara?

"I am bringing it for you to wear to the parade!" Esteban recovers quickly. "And I brought the rest of the jewels so your family would have something to wear as well."

Esteban places the tiara on Elena's head, and then steps back and gasps.

You look just like your mother.

I do?

A distant burst of fanfare interrupts the moment, and Elena shakes herself as if coming out of a trance.

"We should go, they're waiting." She leans in and gives him a kiss on the cheek as she leaves for the courtyard.

The Carnaval parade is being held at Castillo Park in the City of Avalor.

Elena bursts out of the castle and heads straight for the floats. Victor notices that she's wearing the tiara.

Elena often gets help from her best friend Mateo, a young wizard who is Alcazar's grandson.

> What is she doing with the tiara?

An angry Carla goes to join Elena on the float, while Victor heads over to Esteban to see what went wrong with their master plan.

I told you to steal the jewels!

I did. But she caught me.

When Elena was trapped in the Amulet of Avalor, some of the magic was transferred to her. She doesn't yet know the extent of her powers.

"She's handing them out like candy!" Victor whispers. Elena puts a necklace on her grandmother as she laughs with her family.

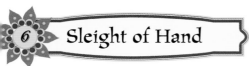

Victor is still furious, and he pokes Esteban in the chest.

"You need to get those jewels back, El Segundo. Or I will tell them *what you did*."

"How am I supposed to do that? They're wearing them!" Esteban protests. At that, Victor smiles.

"The way we used to do it. Our sleight-of-hand tricks! I'll create a distraction."

On the float, Elena hands out the rest of the Crown Jewels to the family. She places a jeweled bracelet on Isabel's wrist, smiling at her.

"Mami wore this bracelet on your tenth birthday, remember?" Elena says.

"Uh-huh!" Isabel says, beaming.

Esteban overhears them as he boards the float with the family and is overcome with guilt.

"Mijito!" Luisa exclaims. "It was so sweet of you to think to bring out the jewels for the parade!"

As the family gets settled, Victor suddenly leaps into the driver's seat on the front cart. He grabs the reins for the horses and snaps them rapidly.

The horses rear and take off!

Caught off guard, the whole family jerks backward as the cart speeds off down the road to the parade.

Ándale means "come on" in Spanish.

¡Ándale!

As the cart takes off, the float is jostled heavily. Esteban is tossed against Luisa, and realizes he has an opportunity to steal back the jewels for Victor.

Esteban put his arms around Luisa and sneakily lifts the jewels from her neck under the guise of helping her steady herself.

Abuela means *grandmother* in Spanish.

Hang on, Abuela, I've got you!

The two-cart float rockets down the hill at top speed! It skids around corners and bounces over potholes, but Victor only urges the horses forward faster.

Esteban pretends to steady Francisco and hold Isabel's hand throughout the turbulent ride, but he's actually taking the opportunity to steal the jewels from them.

Luisa yells to Victor at the front cart, "Victor, slow down! It's not a race!"

BANG! They hit a huge bump, and bounce right out of their seats!

As the family bumps along the road on their way to the parade, Elena notices the beak starting to come loose from the phoenix in the front cart! She tries to get Isabel's attention, but the cart is making such a racket that no one can hear her.

Deciding to fix it herself, Elena shimmies up the neck of the phoenix and attempts to stick the beak back on the bird.

Elena likes to handle problems herself when they come up instead of making others do things for her.

Esteban joins Victor in the front cart and says, "That is it. I have them all."

He deposits the jewels from his satchel into Victor's waiting hands, but is soon interrupted by a shriek from Carla.

Two of the most popular dances in Avalor are the samba and the tango.

No you don't! The tiara!

"It's on her head! There is no way to take it without everyone seeing," hisses Esteban angrily.

Victor sighs. "Get rid of the other cart, Carla."

Stomping over to the link between the two carts, Carla removes the pin that connects the carts, and the rear cart begins to stutter and slow.

As the carts disconnect, Carla leans out and shoves the rear cart with her foot, pushing it away even farther.

Hey! She unhooked our float!

The library at the palace is full of priceless ancient books. Isabel loves to read!

Victor takes the satchel of jewels from Esteban and points to the tiara Elena is wearing.

Get that tiara!

Carla starts scaling the neck of the phoenix where Elena is clinging. Elena gasps, realizing what is happening, and starts to back away.

The royal palace sits atop a hill that overlooks all of Avalor, a city bright with color!

The two out-of-control carts approach a bend in the road. Victor steers right while the untethered cart with the rest of Elena's family flies straight into a meadow!

AAAAHHH!

They jostle, bounce, and toss before finally coming to a halt. They let out a sigh of relief at the end of their bumpy ride, but still worry for Elena and Esteban.

The family picks themselves up from the floor of the cart and groan at their bumps and bruises.

"I think Elena and Esteban are in trouble," Luisa says. "We have to help them, Francisco."

Francisco leaps up with surprising energy and says, "Yes! Let's go!"

49

Meanwhile, the cart with Elena and Esteban in it speeds down the path toward the city, and Elena is struggling to hang on as Carla continues to climb up the phoenix neck to grab the tiara off of Elena's head.

There's no way I'm letting you have my mother's tiara!

Elena's grandmother Luisa is adept at forging compromises between her family members due to her kind nature.

Esteban pleads with Victor, "You already have enough jewels. Just take them and go."

Victor leans in close to Esteban and hisses, "The tiara is the only piece that matters. We're not leaving without it."

"Then you are not leaving at all. I'm finally going to do what I should have done before—the right thing," Esteban replies.

Esteban leaps into the driver's seat and yanks the reins away from Victor. He pulls hard on the reins and yells, "WHOOAA!" The horses shudder to a stop.

Elena is called the Crown Princess because she is only sixteen and not yet old enough to rule by herself. Her official coronation will happen when she turns twenty.

Victor growls and steps aggressively toward Esteban.

"I'm warning you, I'll tell her everything!" he threatens.

Esteban hesitates and looks at Elena, who looks back at him, confused.

Shoring up his courage, Esteban squares his jaw and looks Victor dead in the eye.

Until Elena comes of age, Esteban helps her as part of the Grand Council.

Do what you must.

Victor laughs in disbelief, and calls up to Elena, still clinging to the top of the phoenix. "Princess! It's about time you knew the truth about your dear cousin Esteban!"

"He made a secret deal with Shuriki to help her invade Avalor. He betrayed your family. *That* is how he stayed in power while the rest of us suffered," Victor says sharply.

Elena looks at the two men, shocked. Esteban looks miserable and full of guilt.

When Shuriki invaded Avalor, she cast a spell that made Elena's parents vanish, and then she took over the kingdom.

Still stunned by Victor's accusation, Elena
doesn't notice Carla sneakily continuing her
climb to the top of the phoenix until it's too
late! The two-faced señorita snatches the
tiara from Elena's head and tosses it down
to her father.

"Here you go, Papá!" Carla shouts.

"Gracias, Carla!" Victor laughs.

Enraged, Esteban lunges at Victor, reaching for the tiara.

"No!" Esteban cries.

Victor easily sidesteps Esteban, and when he stumbles, Victor grabs him by the shirt and shoves him into an open hatch, shoving him inside the body of the papier-mâché phoenix.

"Esteban!" Elena shouts.

Victor grabs Elena, too, and throws her into the body of the phoenix with Esteban.

Victor sneers at Esteban with a hand on the door to the hatch.

"Poor El Segundo. You lose again, old friend," he says.

Victor closes the door to the hatch with a slam and latches it shut. Elena leaps to her feet and shoves at the door, trying desperately to push it open.

They locked it!

After making sure the latch is secure, Carla and Esteban unhook the horses from the cart and mount up.

The thieves take off on the stolen horses and head for the heart of the city with all the jewels . . . and the tiara.

¡Ándale!

Trapped in the phoenix float, Esteban sits with his head hanging low. Elena paces restlessly, looking for a way out. Once again she pushes at the seams of the panels, desperately looking for a way out, but the hatch won't budge.

"It's no use! We're stuck in here!" Elena cries, hitting the inside of the float.

When Elena slumps back down next to him, Esteban clears his throat and says:

Elena, about what Victor said . . .

There's nothing to say, Esteban.

"I know Victor was just lying to distract us," Elena continues, scoffing, "Like you'd ever do anything to hurt your own family."

Esteban's eyes widen as he realizes that Elena does not believe Victor. Seeing an opportunity to stay in her good graces, he doesn't correct her.

Elena always trusts her heart—it usually knows where to lead her.

Testing the waters with Elena's forgiveness, Esteban tentatively states:

I do feel guilty for serving Shuriki all those years, though.

You had no choice.

Elena leans close and speaks firmly to her beloved cousin.

"Don't feel guilty for doing what you had to do to survive. When the time came, you stood up to Shuriki and helped us defeat her. You tried to stop Victor just minutes ago. You stood by family when it counted."

Elena sits down beside Esteban and says softly, "It's time to put the past behind you. You can't change what you did before, but you can change what you do next."

You're right, Elena, I can.

Esteban gets up suddenly and starts pacing. He looks determined.

"We must get out of here. We cannot let them get away with this!" He tries to shove open the door, hard, but it doesn't budge. All he succeeds in doing is rocking the float back and forth.

Esteban was a picky eater when he was younger and would only eat his food if his grandparents pretended the spoon was a jaquin flying around.

Aye! Why did Isabel have to make this thing so strong?

He kicks the door in frustration, and the phoenix beak breaks off the head once again, which causes a stream of light to shine on the floor where he and Elena stand.

Except for the beak!

Elena scrambles up the inside of the neck of the phoenix, grasping at the sides to keep from sliding down.

As she nears the top, she squeezes through the head and peeks out from the hole the beak left behind when it fell.

Elena peers out from the hole and sees a road winding down the hillside toward town. She sees Victor and Carla racing two horses on the road, and they're heading right for the heart of the city.

Elena and her family love to sing and play music, and Elena has her own beautifully painted guitar!

"I can see Carla and Victor! They're getting away!" Elena cries. She struggles to move her shoulders, but the hole where the beak fell off is too small for her to fit through.

I can't get out of this thing—the space is too tight!

Determined, Elena squares her jaw and tries again, moving her shoulders and wiggling as much as possible to try and squeeze out of the space.

Esteban watches as Elena tries to fit through the head and notices that the float is rocking along with Elena's movements.

He leans to one side, and the float rocks that way.

Then he leans to the other side and the float rocks the other way. "Elena! I know how we can catch up to them!" he exclaims.

Elena pokes her head down to look at Esteban.

What should I do?

Help me get this float moving!

They begin to rock the float back and forth, rushing from one side of the float to the other.

Just a few more times!

The cousins shove at the left side of the float, wincing as the wooden frame creaks with their efforts. With one final push, they manage to get the float to teeter at the edge of the hill and then start to travel downward!

Papier-mâché feathers rustling in the wind, the phoenix float makes its way down the dirt path and after the thieves. Rocks and holes in the road cause the isolated cart to totter and shake. Esteban and Elena grip the edges of the inside of the float, trying not to fall.

We did it!

"Alright, now we are moving!" Esteban exclaims.

"Quick, climb back up the neck. One of us needs to see where we're going!" Esteban tells Elena.

"You've got it, cousin," Elena answers, grinning. She grasps the frame of the neck and clings tight as she starts to climb up. It's a tight squeeze in her Carnaval gown, but Elena is not one to back away from a challenge! It takes Elena no time at all to reach the top of the head.

Polleras are wide, ruffled skirts worn by women for traditional celebrations in Latin America. They are often colorful, with geometric patterns.

Victor and Carla race down the road, but have to pull up short as the first float of many exits the park in front of them. Between the float and the crowd, the street is completely blocked by the festivities of Carnaval!

How do we get around all of this traffic?

"I don't know," Victor answers, glaring at the parade.

The phoenix float is in hot pursuit of the thieves! It thunders downhill toward town at a breakneck speed. Elena pokes her head out of the hole where the beak fell off, acting as a lookout for Esteban.

Seeing a curve to the left ahead, Elena shouts:

In Avalor, piñatas are used for celebrations like Christmas (Navidad).

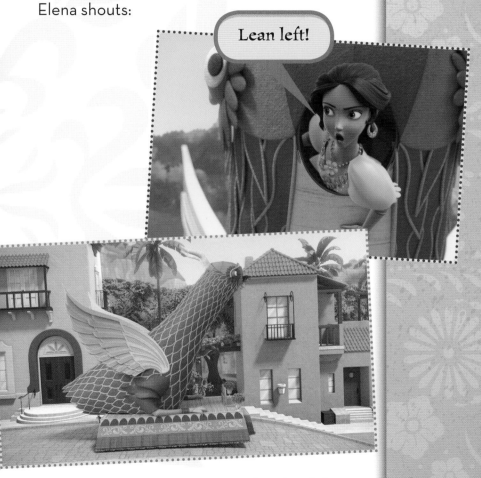

Lean left!

Esteban scrambles to the left side of the bird and leans, making the big float whip around the curve with ease.

Elena peers out of the phoenix head, squinting into the bright sunlight as she tries to focus on searching the road for Carla and Victor. The rattle and bounce of the cart attempts to dislodge her at every turn, but she hangs on tightly! Elena is so preoccupied with staying on that she almost misses the next sharp curve. Gasping, she warns:

Hard to the right, Esteban!

That was close!

Victor and Carla are getting restless. The parade keeps stopping so Avalorans can greet each other and so that little children can come up close to see the floats being driven into town.

As he tries to urge his horse to go faster as it plods along behind the parade, Victor happens to glance over his shoulder, and his eyes widen as he spots the royal phoenix float thundering down the hill!

The claves are a pair of wooden dowels, often used in samba music.

Carla!
They're coming!

Carla springs into action, helping her father twist and turn past the heavy foot traffic of the parade-goers.

"How did they get that cart moving again if they were trapped inside?" demands Victor.

Carla just shrugs angrily, yelling at people to get out of their way. Victor and Carla weave around the various floats and head toward the entrance of the park, trying to escape unnoticed by the royal float.

Elena, peeks out of the phoenix, spots them, and yells at Esteban to hang a hard left.

Lean left now! We can still catch them!

Elena and Esteban come hurtling down into the thick of the parade preparations in their rickety cart, with Elena peeking out from the phoenix's beak. Elena spots Victor and Carla as they pass a Maruvian Temple Float full of Avalorans. The float is colorful and loud with the din of singing and cheering voices, but Elena tries to be heard anyway.

Thieves! Stop them!

One of the parading Avalorans on top of the Maruvian Temple float hears Elena's cry and looks to where she is pointing. He gasps when he sees the escaping Victor and Carla, and turns to shout to the driver of his float: "Change directions, quickly!"

Elena takes her role as Crown Princess very seriously, as she wants to be as wise and noble of a leader as her father, King Raul.

The Crown Princess needs us!

With Esteban's leaning and Elena's navigating, the phoenix float is catching up to the thieves! Victor looks behind him and gasps as he sees the royals gaining on him and his daughter.

Follow me!

Together, they gallop toward a nearby stone wall that looks low enough for their horses to jump over.

Elena notices too late that the thieves are putting them in the path of the stone wall, and warns Esteban.

Uh-oh. Brace yourself, Esteban!

Brace myself? Why?

With a crash, the phoenix float hits the low wall and the wheels stop short. But the momentum makes the papier-mâché phoenix come right off the cart and launch over the wall! The royal phoenix has taken flight!

The wings of the phoenix float catch the wind, and it soars well over the stone wall and gains on the escaping thieves. The shadow of the phoenix looms directly over Victor and Carla as they gallop away. The horses are so frightened that they buck off their riders.

The float breaks apart when it hits the ground, and Elena and Esteban stumble out of it, finally free.

Because Elena's royal duties as a Crown Princess keep her busy, she makes sure to share meals with her family so she can still spend time with them.

Faced with Elena and Esteban, Victor and Carla quickly run to the wall and vault back over the side.

They prepare to run through the parade again, only to be faced with a giant crowd of Avalorans the minute they touch down on the other side of the wall.

The thieves are truly trapped!

12 The King of the Carnaval

Victor tries to make a break for it, but
Luisa, Francisco, Armando, and Isabel have
finally caught up, and they block his path.
Esteban steps up to Victor and takes
back his satchel with the family's jewels.

I'll take those,
old friend.

The crowd of Avalorans parts as the Captain of the Guard and one of his squads breaks through to confront the thieves.

Elena strides forward to address him, saying:

Captain! Remove these thieves from our kingdom— and see that they never return!

Yes, your majesty.

82

Later that day, a Royal Guard prisoner wagon rattles out of the park. With bars on the windows and a guard at each corner, the prisoners have no chance at escape.

Inside, Victor and Carla sit inside on hard benches, stone-faced.

What do we do now? We need that tiara.

We will find another way, Carla. I assure you, Avalor has not heard the last of us.

Back at the park, the Royal Family surveys the damage done to the phoenix float. Nervous, Esteban turns to Isabel and apologizes, "I am sorry about your float, Isabel."

"Are you kidding? It almost flew! Which gives me a great idea for next year!" Isabel replies eagerly.

"Oh dear," Francisco says.

Sifting through the now-retrieved satchel, Esteban pulls out the tiara and places it carefully on Elena's head. He smiles at her, saying:

This is where your mother's tiara belongs.

Thank you, Esteban. I wish we had something to give you.

Isabel brightens as she spots the paper Carnaval crown among the wreckage of the battered float. It's a little bit lopsided, but still mostly intact.

> **We do have something to give you, Esteban!**

Elena beams, brushing off the crown and putting it on Esteban's head.

"You said you weren't worthy of this honor. But I think you've earned the right to wear the crown," Elena says warmly.

Elena smiles at Esteban and
announces to the crowd:

Chancellor Esteban!
I hereby proclaim you
King of the Carnaval!

"Well, Esteban," Elena continues, "Would you like to do the honors?"

"Nothing would please me more," he replies, smiling.

The crowd cheers, the band blasts, and Elena and Esteban lock arms and join their family for an amazing Carnaval!

Let the Carnaval Parade begin!